For Patricia, Oreo, and the Pépette
— J.-P. A.-V.

To Gabriel
— O. T.

First published in the United States in 2009 by Chronicle Books LLC.

Text © 2006 by Jean-Philippe Arrou-Vignod.
Illustrations © 2006 by Olivier Tallec.
Translation © 2009 by Chronicle Books LLC.
Originally published in France in 2006 by Gallimard Jeunesse under the title
Rita et Machin.

North American type design by Natalie Davis.
Typeset in The Serif Semi Light.
Manufactured in China.

Library of Congress Cataloging-in-Publication Data
Arrou-Vignod, Jean-Philippe, 1958–
[Rita et Machin. English]
Rita and Whatsit / by Jean-Philippe Arrou-Vignod ; illustrated by Olivier
Tallec.
p. cm.
Summary: Rita is surprised to receive a dog for her birthday, and she is even
more shocked when she discovers that the dog can talk.
ISBN 978-0-8118-6550-0
[1. Dogs—Fiction.] I. Tallec, Olivier, ill. II. Title.
PZ7.A74339Ri 2009
[E]—dc22
2008030733

10 9 8 7 6 5 4 3 2 1

Chronicle Books LLC
680 Second Street, San Francisco, California 94107

www.chroniclekids.com

ou-VIGNOD Illustrated by OLIVIER TALLEC

chronicle books · san francisco

It was her birthday, but Rita was in a bad mood.

She had decided that nothing would
please her. Not the cake or the presents.
Everything was *too*.

Too big,

too small,

too medium . . .

In the corner, one present
began to jiggle.

Suddenly, the present jumped up
and bounced across the floor.

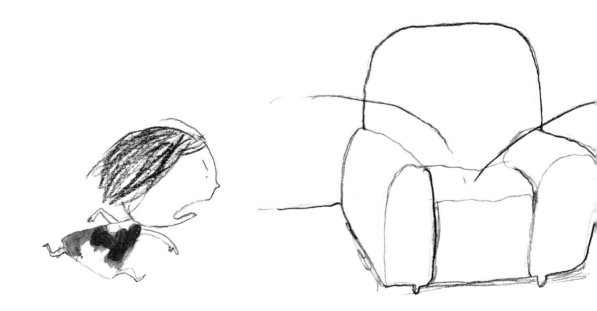

"Get back here, present, or you'll regret it!" yelled Rita.

She'd never seen a present that ran
away before.

And guess what she found inside?

A fuzzy little dog. The present held very still and looked at her.

"I'm warning you," said Rita, "if you're another stuffed animal, you're going in the trash!"

The dog didn't say a word. He got up and scooted around a corner. *Doesn't* look *like a stuffed animal,* thought Rita.

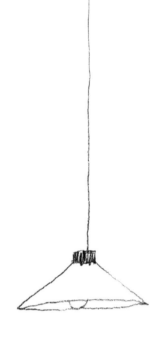

Rita made her new pet a snack.
She brought him

a large slice of cake,
a bowl of milk,
and two candies.

"Are you hungry, little dog? I'm warning you, if you don't stop hiding, I'll pack you back up in your box!"

The dog disappeared.

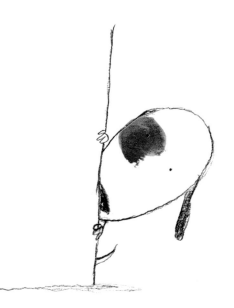

Where did he go?

"Get back here right now, little dog! If you want me to keep you, you need a name. Maybe I'll call you Washington, or Lincoln."

Rita scratched her head.

"No, with names like those, you'd always want to be in charge. How about I call you Kneesock? Do you even care what I name you?"

Rita shook, scratched, and tickled the dog.

"You'd better not start snoring! We're just getting to know each other! If you keep lying there, I'll call you Floormop! And who wants a dog called Floormop?"

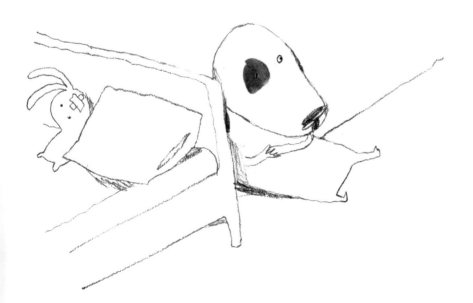

"I know!" cried Rita. "What if I just call you Whatsit?
It's the perfect name for a dog without a name."

"That's perfect," said the dog. "Shake."

Rita could hardly believe her ears.
"You *talk*, Whatsit?"

"Only when necessary," said the dog.

"Whatsit, I have a feeling we're going to be great friends."

"Me too," said Whatsit. "Could I borrow some pajamas?"

Rita's birthday is over and everything is quiet.
Is she still in a bad mood? No, she's fast asleep.

She and Whatsit opened all the presents
and played with all the toys.

What a birthday! Tomorrow there
will be even more fun things to do.

But for now, shh!
Rita has a brand-new friend.